How COOL is that?!

So when it was time for the school talent show, they shone like
STARS!

and they
practised...

and they
PRACTISED...

They practised . . .

Then they started jamming and singing
and this was their song . . .

She wanted to write
what she wanted to sing.

Miss Butler helped her to
choose the words.

And suddenly Abigail **DID** want to write.

"Ooh! We need a singer for our band," said Ruby. "Will you join us?"

Abigail could have BURST with pride!

But instead, Miss Butler smiled.

"Wow, Abi!" she said. "You have such a strong voice! You're a natural born singer."

"Back to the calming down room,"
thought Abigail . . .

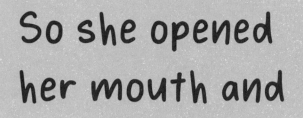

So she opened
her mouth and

Abigail wanted to join in . . .

. . . but she didn't know how to.

The guitar looked fun but the strings hurt Abigail's fingers.

Rex didn't care! He played it like a pro.

Ruby was drumming
a beat all of her own.

She had terrific rhythm.

Abigail just couldn't
keep up.

Lina was playing the recorder.

She was BRILLIANT!

"I'll never be as good . . ."
thought Abigail.

"There you are, Abigail! Come and join us," said Miss Butler.

She didn't seem cross at all.

"Choose any instrument you like."

The next class was MUSIC.
She had never been to a Music class before . . .

The lady in the calming down room was kind but Abigail did not feel like talking.

Abigail was taken to the
calming down room.

Teacher **wasn't** pleased.

and fiddling with **Lottie's** hair!

Lottie didn't like it but Abigail
thought it was funny.

She wanted to
do scribbling . . .

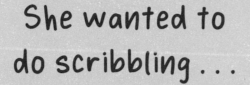

and fiddling with
her hair . . .

It wasn't a good day. Abigail was restless.

She didn't want to do writing.

LOUD!

ROSE ROBBINS

Scallywag Press Ltd

LONDON

For my brother Merlin

Thank you to Dr Rebecca Butler who advised me on this book,
and is the inspiration for the character of "Miss Butler".

First published in Great Britain in 2021 by Scallywag Press Ltd,
10 Sutherland Row, London SW1V 4JT.

Copyright © 2021 by Rose Robbins

The rights of Rose Robbins to be identified as the author and illustrator of this work have been asserted by her
in accordance with the Copyright, Designs and Patents Act, 1988.

Art Direction and design by Sarah Finan

Printed in Malaysia by Tien Wah Press

001

British Library Cataloguing in Publication Data available.

ISBN 978-1-912650-56-9

LOUD!

A book to share from
Scallywag Press